The Tinder Box

Based on a story by
Hans Christian Andersen

Retold by Russell Punter
Illustrated by Annette Marnat

Reading consultant: Alison Kelly

What is a tinder box?

Tinder boxes were used for starting fires before matches were invented. Inside each box was a flintstone, a piece of steel and some cloth or straw (tinder).

Hitting the steel with the flint made sparks. The sparks set light to the tinder. The tinder could be used to set light to firewood or candles.

Contents

Chapter 1

The witch's bargain

A long, long time ago, a poor soldier named Tom was marching home after a battle.

Suddenly, a witch leaped out from behind a bush. "Would you like to be rich?" she asked.

"Huh?" said Tom in surprise. "Um, who wouldn't?"

The witch pointed to a hollow tree. "Beneath that tree is a cave with three treasure rooms."

Tom's eyes lit up. "Treasure?"

"In the first room," said the witch, "is a chest piled high with copper coins."

"In the second is a chest full of silver. The chest in the third room is crammed with gold."

"Wow!" said Tom.

"You'll have to be careful,"
the witch warned. "Each chest
is guarded by a fierce dog."

"Ha! I'm a soldier," Tom
said. "I can defend myself."

"You won't need to," said the witch, untying the apron around her waist. "Place the dogs on this, and they won't harm you."

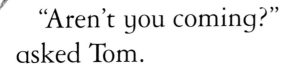

"Aren't you coming?" asked Tom.

"That cave is full of fireflies," shuddered the old woman. "Just one touch is deadly to a witch."

"I can see why you need my help," said Tom. "I suppose you want half the treasure?"

"It's all yours," the witch
replied, "if you bring me an old
tinder box you'll find there."

Tom grinned and the
witch handed him a rope.
"All right soldier," she
ordered. "Get climbing!"

11

Chapter 2

Treasure galore

In no time at all, Tom had reached the top of the tree. He clambered inside the trunk and lowered himself down.

The further Tom went, the darker it got. But after a while, he saw a golden glow.

Tom dropped into a cavern,
lit by dozens of shimmering
fireflies. On one wall were
three carved doors.

Those must be
the treasure
rooms.

Tom laid his backpack on
the ground and pulled open the
first door.

It swung open with a
creak... Tom crept inside.

A chest stood in the middle of the room. Perched on top was a dog with eyes as big as tea cups.

Tom took out the apron. "I hope this works," he thought, spreading it on the floor.

He picked up the dog as gently as he could and rested it on the apron.

To Tom's surprise, the fierce-looking dog snuggled down.

"Whew!" gasped Tom. "Now for the chest."

He opened the lid and a stream of shiny copper coins tumbled out.

I'm rich!

Tom stuffed as many coins as he could into his hat. Then he put the dog back on the chest and went to the next room.

There, seated on a bigger chest, was a dog with eyes as large as saucers.

Once again, Tom laid the apron on the floor and sat the dog on top.

He tugged open the chest
and hundreds of sparkly silver
coins poured out.

I'm really rich!

His pockets bulging with
silver, Tom put the dog back
and clinked into the last room.

A dog with eyes as big as
dinner plates was resting on
the biggest chest of all.

Tom gulped.

But once more, the dog was
completely calm as Tom placed
it on the apron.

He heaved open the chest
and thousands of glittering
gold coins cascaded out.

I'm rich beyond
my dreams!

He fetched his backpack from
the cavern and filled it with
gold. Then he replaced the dog.

Tom was on his way out,
when he remembered the
witch's request.

He searched the cave until
he found the tinder box, half
hidden between two rocks.

Soon, he was back outside.
"Give me the box!" shrieked
the witch. As she ran forward,
a firefly buzzed out of Tom's
backpack.

"Nooo!" she screeched. It was
too late.

The tiny bug landed on her nose and WHOOSH! The witch vanished in a puff of smoke.

Aaarggh!

"Poor witch," sighed Tom, but there was nothing he could do.

Chapter 3

The secret of the tinder box

Jangling loudly, Tom marched to the nearby town and booked into the most expensive hotel.

"Here you are," he said, handing over a pile of coins. "Please bring me the tastiest food on your menu."

At first, Tom led a fine life.
But he had a kind heart, and
gave away most of his fortune
to the poor.

Thank you, sir!

It wasn't long before every
coin was spent. All Tom had
left was the brass tinder box.

He moved out of the hotel's best room. Now he slept in the cramped, cold attic.

Brrrrr! I'm freezing.

"I'll light a candle to keep warm," he thought, opening the tinder box.

He struck the steel once with the flint. There was a flash of sparks...

...the door flew open and in bounded a dog with eyes as big as tea cups.

"It's the dog from the cave," cried Tom in amazement.

"What is your command, master?" barked the dog.

Tom thought for a moment. "Well, I could really use some money..." he began.

The dog raced from the room and returned in seconds, with a bulging bag of coins.

"So that's why the witch wanted the tinder box," said Tom. "Now I wonder..."

He struck the steel twice and the dog with eyes as big as saucers appeared. Three strikes brought the dog with eyes as large as dinner plates.

This tinder box will come in very useful...

Chapter 4

Tom meets a princess

Tom had enough money to buy a huge house in the middle of town. One morning, a grand coach rode past.

The king and queen sat
inside, but no one cheered or
even looked at them.

"No one likes those two,"
explained Tom's maid.
"Why?" asked Tom.

"They keep their daughter, Princess Rose, locked up in the palace," said the maid. "The king won't let anyone see her."

"*I'd* like to see her," thought Tom, "if only for a moment. And I think I know how."

That night, he took out the
tinder box and struck the steel.
The dog with eyes as big as
tea cups padded into the room.

What is your command?

Please bring Princess Rose here.

The dog barked and ran off.
Moments later, he was back
with a sleepy princess.

37

As soon as he saw her, Tom fell in love. At dawn, the dog carried Princess Rose home.

"I had a strange dream last night," Rose told her parents, that morning. "A huge dog carried me to a grand house."

"Humph!" snorted the king.
"I just hope it *was* a dream."
"Let's find out," said the queen.

She filled a silk bag with
flour. As the princess slept, the
queen tied the bag to her, and
cut a tiny hole in its side.

That night, the dog carried the princess to Tom's house again. But this time, they left a trail behind.

The next morning, the king
followed the trail.

"No one sees the princess,"
the king roared at Tom. "You
will die at dawn!"

Chapter 5

Rescue!

Tom was flung into a damp,
dark prison cell. He lay awake
all night thinking of Rose.

Just before dawn, his maid appeared outside.

"I've come to say goodbye, sir," she sobbed.

I have an idea.

"Please run home and get my tinder box," whispered Tom.

Minutes later, the maid returned and passed the box through the bars.

As the sun rose, the king's guards marched Tom outside. The crowd lining the streets felt sorry for him.

"Silence!" hissed the queen. "Yes, be quiet!" yelled the king. "Or you're all next."

At that moment, Tom whipped out the tinder box. He struck the steel once, twice, then three times.

The three dogs from the cave barged through the crowd.

"Save me from the king and queen!" cried Tom.

With a blood-chilling howl, the dogs chased the pair from the kingdom.

Tom rushed to free Rose and asked her to be his wife.

They were married before the week was out.

"Hooray!" cheered the crowd and Tom's three loyal dogs barked as if to agree.

About the story

The original version of *The Tinder Box* was published in 1835. It was one of the first fairy tales written by Hans Christian Andersen (1805-1875), who was the son of a Danish shoemaker. He went on to write many more stories, including *The Emperor's New Clothes, The Princess and the Pea* and *The Little Mermaid.*

Series editor: Lesley Sims

First published in 2014 by Usborne Publishing Ltd., Usborne House, 83-85 Saffron Hill, London EC1N 8RT, England. www.usborne.com
Copyright © 2014 Usborne Publishing Ltd.